Bestie Day

Read More
Trillium Sisters
Stories!

Trillium Sisters

Bestie Day

Laura Brown and Elly Kramer

Illustrated by Sarah Mensinga

PIXEL✛INK

PIXEL+INK

Text copyright © 2021 by Laura Brown and Elly Kramer

Interior illustrations copyright © 2021 by TGM Development Corp.

Pixel+Ink is a division of TGM Development Corp.

Printed and bound in April 2021 at Maple Press, York, PA, U.S.A.

Book design by Yaffa Jaskoll

www.pixelandinkbooks.com

Library of Congress Control Number: 2020944064

Hardcover ISBN 978-1-64595-016-5

Paperback ISBN 978-1-64595-023-3

eBook ISBN 978-1-64595-071-4

First Edition

1 3 5 7 9 10 8 6 4 2

For our fathers, Jon and Arnold,
who inspired Dr. J.A., and our mothers,
Marian and Anne, who taught us to
be strong sisters.
—L.B. and E.K.

CHAPTER 1

As the morning sun poured into the tree house, Emmy, Giselle, and Clare looked through the bins in their craft room. It was Bestie Day, the holiday when everyone on Trillium Mountain celebrated their besties. As sisters *and* best friends, the triplets wanted to make one another perfect presents.

"Ugh," said Emmy. "Markers? Glitter

glue? Pipe cleaners? None of this feels special enough for Bestie Day gifts."

Giselle fiddled with the pet rocks they had made last year. "Yeah, we're eight now. This year, our gifts have to really rock!"

Clare giggled. "I know! Let's hike into the forest. We're old enough to go alone and there's tons of cool stuff there to use for crafts."

"Sounds fun," agreed Emmy. "But we still have to figure out exactly what we're making."

Clare tucked her hair behind a pink headband she had decorated with tiny flowers. It gave her an idea. "How about matching headbands? We can dress them up with pretty things we find, like I did with this one."

Giselle eyed Clare's collection of head-bands. It covered an entire shelf. "Yeah, you definitely need another one," she teased.

"Maybe *I* don't, but *you* do!" Clare laughed, then tweaked Giselle's messy ponytail.

Giselle giggled. "We all know hair's not my thing."

"C'mere," said Clare. "I'll French braid it for you."

Clare started to brush out Giselle's hair while Emmy straightened the lanyard that held her green trillium charm around her neck.

"I wish we could think of something as special as these trillium charms to give one another," said Emmy.

Clare jumped to her feet. "Trilliums—that's it! What if we collect real trillium petals in the forest and use *them* to make gifts for Bestie Day!"

"Homemade trillium gifts? That's perfect, Clare!" said Emmy.

"One hundred percent!" agreed Giselle. "I mean, trilliums are so important to us, they're like . . . our . . . our mascot!"

And it was true. Eight years ago, when their father had found the sisters as babies in the forest, they each had a trillium petal charm by their side. Dad had carefully kept the charms for his daughters. A few months ago when they turned eight, he had returned them, confident they were mature enough to care for the precious enamel charms.

The triplets had made the charms into jewelry so they'd never be without them. Clare had crafted her hot pink charm into an earring. Giselle had turned her blue charm into an anklet. And Emmy hung her green petal charm around her neck. With three petals, the trillium flower was a triplet, just like they were. That's why they called each other "Trills" and saw the flowers as their symbol.

With the Bestie Day gifts settled, the girls scrambled down the tree house ladder. Zee, their younger brother, was already in the kitchen feeding Fluffy. Suddenly, the wolf pup started to bark. He ran to the kitchen door wagging his tail furiously. Mrs. Lilienstern, their neighbor, waved from the kitchen stoop. "Happy Bestie Day!" she called.

"Same to you!" said the triplets' father, Dr. J.A. "Come in, Lillian! Would you like some ice-cold daisy juice?"

"Thanks, John Arnold, but I haven't got time. I'm on my way to give Mayor Mae her Bestie Day gift," said Mrs. Lilienstern. "But first, I had to show you what she made *me*!" She held up a piece of carved wood. It looked like a nose.

"She gave you . . . a . . . nose?" said Zee.

"Yes! But, not just any nose! This one keeps me from losing my eyeglasses at home.

Let me show you," said Mrs. Lilienstern. She rummaged through her bag. "Ugh, where *are* my glasses?!"

"On your head!" said Zee.

Mrs. Lilienstern laughed . "See why I need it?" She rested her glasses on the wooden carving and suddenly it looked like a face.

"Mayor Mae sure knows what you need," said Zee.

"A Bestie always does," said Mrs. Lilienstern. "Okay, gotta go! Have the best Bestie Day!" She flew out of the kitchen, shutting the door behind her.

"Dad, what are you and Zee doing for Bestie Day?" asked Emmy.

"We're going to play in Aspen Grove, near

the top of the mountain," said Dr. J.A.

"Daddy, can we play Lighthouse at the Grove? Can we? Can we?" said Zee. He bounced in his chair.

Lighthouse was Zee's favorite game. The goal was to sneak through the forest and reach one of the trees—the "lighthouse"—without the lighthouse keeper seeing you. With its closely knit trees to hide behind, Aspen Grove was the perfect place to play the game.

"We can try, but Lighthouse is better with more people," said Dr. J.A.

"Yup, if the keeper only has to guard the lighthouse from one person, it's too easy," agreed Giselle.

"But I have other fun for us!" said Dr. J.A. He held up his day pack. It was stuffed with balls, ropes, a frisbee, a jar of bubbles, even a set of checkers.

"Whoa!" cried Zee. He started shoveling the remaining cereal into his mouth as fast as he could.

Dr. J.A. placed a pitcher of daisy juice on the table. "And how about my favorite triplet

Besties? What are you doing today?"

"We're making gifts like always, Dad," said Clare. "But this year, we're going to the forest to collect trillium petals for them."

"I give that a green thumbs-up!" said Dr. J.A. "Just make sure you only collect *fallen* petals."

"We know, Dad," said Giselle. "We'd never pick a healthy wildflower, only petals that have fallen off. The plant doesn't need those anymore."

"That's my girl," said Dr. J.A. "Head to the flower field. There'll be plenty of freshly fallen petals there."

"That's the plan, Dad!" said Clare. "Great minds . . ."

". . . are mighty fine!" finished her dad. He laughed at his own joke.

Giselle put her bowl in the sink. "I'll go pack our gear."

"I'll help," said Clare as she followed Giselle up the ladder.

CHAPTER 2

Emmy remained at the table, stirring her cereal round and round. She was excited to collect trillium petals, but she couldn't stop thinking about when their father had first given them their charms. The day had started so happily, but then something terrible had happened. Zee had accidentally fallen into the river! And then, just when Emmy feared he'd be swept away by the rushing water, their petal charms had combined into a glowing trillium charm and given the girls magic powers to save him!

The magic had been incredible, but the memory of that day nagged at her. She knew so little about the magic. Would their petal charms ever come together to give them power again? And, if they did, then what? Would she and her sisters be brave enough to face another emergency?

"Em?" said Dr. J.A.

Emmy looked up, startled. "Sorry, Dad. I was spacing out," she said.

"I see that," said Dr. J.A. "Everything okay?"

"Yeah, fine. It's just . . . well, I can't stop

thinking about when you gave us our charms. What if there's another emergency like there was that day?"

"Honey, there's no reason why there should be another emergency," he said.

"I know," she replied softly. "It's silly to worry."

"No, I didn't say that. Feelings are never silly. I understand why you're nervous."

Emmy smiled at her dad. He always understood.

"But remember," he continued. "If the charms do join together again, you and your sisters will become an even more powerful team than you already are. Together, you'll be able to handle anything!"

Emmy smiled. "You're right, Dad. I'll have my Besties with me!"

"Always! Now go enjoy!" said Dr. J.A.

Emmy picked up her spoon. The cereal tasted better now. She finished breakfast and then climbed the ladder to join her sisters.

CHAPTER 3

It looked like Giselle had dumped their entire closet onto the bedroom floor. Water bottles, craft supplies, hiking boots, backpacks, and plastic containers were strewn about. The mini'mals, the girl's mini pets, ran through the mess, sniffing it all.

"What happened here?" Emmy giggled.

"Just getting stuff ready," said Giselle. "It's

all going in the packs, don't worry."

Claw, Emmy's bear cub, lifted a plastic bowl in her mouth and dropped it gently in Emmy's lap.

"Thanks, Claw," said Emmy. "But why do we need a plastic bowl?" She handed it to Giselle.

"Whoops!" said Giselle. She wiped the bowl with a soapy cloth. "Bear saliva and perfume definitely don't mix!"

"Perfume?" exclaimed Emmy.

"Yup!" said Giselle. "I figure we'll make perfume from some

of the petals for Clare. Think she'll like that?"

"Definitely not!" said Emmy. "I think she'll *love* it!"

She spied Clare in the craft room. She was fiddling with two square pieces of wood. One lay on top of the other. Four screws in the corners held the wood pieces together. Emmy walked over. "What's that, Clare?"

"A flower press," said Clare. "You put a flower in between the pieces of wood. Then, you tighten these screws so the wood presses together and squeezes the moisture out of the flower. Once the flower's dried, you can keep it forever!"

"Trilltastic!" said Emmy.

"I'm going to press trillium petals and decorate a bookmark for you," said Clare. "Then, we'll all be together, even when you're reading!"

"I *love* that idea!" said Emmy. "Thanks, Clare!"

"Now we just have to figure out what to make for Giselle," said Clare.

Emmy looked around the craft room. Paint, construction paper, ribbons—she didn't see anything just right for her sporty sister.

But then Clare eyed the sewing kit. "Rosy roses!" she cried. She removed a needle and some blue and green thread, then grabbed an old baseball cap Giselle hadn't worn in years off a shelf. "We can make this old cap new by sewing trillium petals on it!" she said.

"So cool, Clare," said Emmy. "How do you *think* of all these things?"

Clare shrugged. "I just let my mind go. And an idea hatches!"

"Well, we are all set," said Emmy. "Just need my bear sling." Emmy lifted the canvas holder off the floor and pulled it on across her body.

"Right, the flower field is too far away for the minis to walk," agreed Clare.

"*Rrrr, rrr, rrr!*" barked Fluffy. He wagged his tail from side to side as fast as it would go.

"*Aroooo!*" went Claw. She stood up on her hind legs.

Soar, Giselle's pet eaglet, snagged a leash in her beak and held it up to Clare.

"Clare, the mini'mals heard you say *W-A-L-K* so they think they're getting one!" said Emmy.

"Aww, sour flowers! I got them all excited." Clare sighed.

"No worries. They love to *ride*, too," said Giselle. She held out a backpack with a little perch in it. "Soar! Come!" she called.

"*Woo! Woo!*" went Soar. She dropped the leash and hopped onto the perch. Giselle lifted the pack and strapped it gently to her back.

Clare whistled for Fluffy, who settled happily into a larger backpack while Emmy scooped up Claw and positioned her in the bear sling.

Then, the girls hopped onto the slide, which ran from the top of the tree house to the bottom, and whooshed down to the yard.

CHAPTER 4

Dr. J.A. was throwing a Frisbee to Zee near the slide exit when he heard the girls coming down. "Heads-up!" he called, as it sailed toward Zee.

"You mean *hands* up!" laughed Giselle. She whizzed out and intercepted the Frisbee. Zee looked at his empty hands with surprise.

"How'd you *do* that, Gelly? Teach me!" begged Zee.

"Can't now. We're leaving for the flower field. I'll show you later," she promised.

"Why don't you just cut flowers from our garden?" said Zee.

"Zee, we don't cut healthy flowers," said Clare.

"Why? We've got lots!" said Zee.

The girls looked at each other. This could

take a minute. They dropped their packs so the mini'mals could play in the yard. Then they walked over to Zee.

"Flowers feed the bees," said Emmy. "That's one reason we never waste them."

"Right," agreed Dr. J.A. "In fact, I planted flowers here to *attract* bees."

"Why would you want more bees?" asked Zee.

"Because the bees help the flowers just as much as the flowers help the bees," said Clare.

Giselle pointed to a bee hovering near a geranium. "That bee is drinking the flower's nectar, Zee. Nectar gives bees the energy to fly."

"Like the juice I drank for breakfast?" said

Zee. He jumped up and down. "That gives me energy to play?"

"Exact-bee!" Emmy laughed. "But that's not all. When bees drink nectar, their bodies get covered in a powder on the flower called pollen. As they fly around, they spread that pollen to other flowers."

"And *that* helps the plants make *new* plants so we get more flowers," said Clare.

"Plus," added Giselle, "if the plant is one that we eat, or one that grows food, then spreading the pollen means we'll have more plants to eat!"

"Huh?" said Zee. "You lost me there."

Emmy pointed to the blueberries growing in a corner of the garden. Three bees drank from its flowers. "As those bees move from flower to flower, they're spreading pollen all over the blueberry bush. That means the bush makes more blueberries."

"Wow!" said Zee. "Thanks, bees! I *love* blueberries!"

Just then, Fluffy ran by.

"*Buzzzzz!*" went the bees.

Startled, Fluffy fell backward and burped.

Clare giggled. "Excuse you!" she said.

Fluffy whimpered.

Clare hugged her pup. "What's wrong, Fluff? Are you scared of the bees? You burp when you're scared."

Fluffy hid his head behind her legs.

"Don't worry, Fluffy! Check this out!" said

Giselle. She skipped around the blueberry plant, but the bees ignored her. "The bees want the yummy nectar, not me! See?"

Fluffy peeked out and watched Giselle. Then he wagged his tail.

"C'mon, boy!" said Clare. She held out the backpack and Fluffy hopped in.

"Good move, Clare. It's time to get buzzing," said their dad.

"To Aspen Grove, Daddy?" said Zee.

"You betcha," said Dr. J.A.

The girls strapped the other pets into place and headed out of the yard, but Dr. J.A. put a hand on Emmy's shoulder to stop her for a moment. "Em, I've got something for you," he said. He pulled a soft leather pouch out of his pocket. It was colored in the exact same shades of pink, blue, and green as their charms.

"What's this, Dad?" she asked.

"It's for you girls. If there's ever another emergency and the petal charms *do* combine, this will keep the trillium charm safe," he said.

"Wow, Dad, thanks!

But what made you think of this?" asked Emmy.

"Someone I love was a little nervous this morning," he said.

Emmy smiled at her dad. She tucked the pouch into her pocket. "Well, I'm not nervous anymore!"

"Neither am I," said Dr. J.A.

"Happy Bestie Day, Dad!" said Emmy. She hugged him tightly. Then they headed out to enjoy the day.

CHAPTER 5

The girls hiked toward the flower field, but it wasn't long before Emmy stopped. "It's so hot, Trills! I need some water," she said.

Clare wiped her face with a bright pink bandana. "Sure is. And the flower field is far away."

Giselle reached back to pet Soar. "Wouldn't it be cool to fly there on Soar like we did

when we had magic powers?"

"The magic made our minis big!" said Clare. "Soar was so maxi, we all fit on her back!"

"I'd love to see the flower field from the air," agreed Emmy. "Imagine how all those blossoms would look from the sky!"

"Like a painting," said Clare. "A million dots of pink, yellow, and purple against a sea of green."

Emmy and Clare closed their eyes.

"Hate to burst your bubble," said Giselle, "but you know Soar can't get big again unless there's an emergency."

Emmy frowned. "Right. That's what would make the charms combine again, if they ever do." She shook her head. "Cool as our powers are, I'm not wishing for another emergency."

"Me neither," agreed Clare.

"Me three-ther." Giselle giggled.

Suddenly, Fluffy's ears pricked up.

"*Weeeeee!*"

Clare tipped her head back to look up. "Oh, hi, Mayor Mae!" she called. "Loved the eye-glass holder bestie gift!"

Mayor Mae whooshed over their heads. Trillium Mountain had a network of zip lines connected to the trees all over the mountain. Anyone could take a swing and zip wherever they needed to be!

"*Thaaank youuuuu!*" Mayor Mae called.

"Wow, that's fast *and* breezy! And it gives me an idea! Let's zip-line to the flower field," said Clare.

"Sounds perfect. Let's do it," said Emmy.

"You guys go. I'll kayak to the field," said Giselle. "That way, we can store the petals under the hood of the kayak so they don't wilt on the way home."

"Okay. Meet you there, sis?" said Clare.

"Yup! If you get to the field before me, get started," said Giselle. "I'll holler for ya when I arrive!" With that, she went to fetch her kayak.

Emmy and Clare headed for the nearest ladder and climbed up to the zip line platform. From there, Emmy lowered herself onto a swing, making sure Claw was secure in her bear sling. Then she held the cable that attached the swing to the zip line in both hands, pushed off the platform with her feet, and sailed over the forest floor. "*Weeeeee!*" she exclaimed.

"*Arooooo!*" went Claw.

Clare and Fluffy followed on their own swing.

"*Wahooo!*" Clare cried.

"*Rarooo!*" howled Fluffy.

They arrived at the flower field in minutes.

Back on the ground, Emmy looked around in awe. "Twinkling tulips!" she said.

"*And* dancing daisies! This is the prettiest I've ever seen the field!" said Clare.

"Everything's in bloom," agreed Emmy.

The mini'mals jumped out of the carrying gear and raced into the field!

"Wait up!" called Clare. She and Emmy ran after their pets.

CHAPTER 6

Deep in the field, Emmy and Clare collected trillium petals. Clare lifted up the bottom of her shirt to make a pocket and dropped the petals inside. Emmy remembered her pouch and put some inside the leather sack.

"Hey, what's that, Em?" said Clare.

"I forgot to show you!" said Emmy. "Dad made this to hold the trillium charm."

"Love it!" said Clare.

"Yeah, the only problem is that when I'm holding it, I only have one hand to collect petals," said Emmy.

"Hmmm . . ." said Clare as she examined the pouch.

"Is another idea hatching?" said Emmy.

"I think so," said Clare. She took off

her headband, threaded it through the pouch holes, and then tied the whole thing around Emmy's waist like a belt.

"Crafty! Thanks, Clare," said Emmy. But suddenly, something caught her eye. "Hey, what's that?" she asked.

Clare saw it, too—something bright orange waving back and forth in the distance. "Maybe it's a flag?" she said.

"Maybe someone needs help?" said Emmy.

"Let's go see," said Clare.

The girls walked toward the spot where they had seen the flash of orange. As they got closer, they recognized some girls they knew from town. Tall and skinny with red curls and freckles, Willy was cutting the largest wildflowers she could find with a clipper big enough to trim a hedge. *Snip, snip, snip!*

"Look, Em!" whispered Clare. A neon orange flyswatter stuck out of Willy's back pocket.

Abby, rounder and shorter than Willy

with glossy black hair that hung down her back, followed Willy, catching the flowers that she had cut. Then Abby gingerly placed them on a pile to the side.

"Buzzz!" Bees hovered near the pile of freshly cut flowers.

Willy turned toward the buzzing. "Bug off, bugs!" she yelled. She grabbed the swatter and swung it.

Emmy waved her hands. "No! Please, stop!" she called. She ran toward Willy.

Willy shielded her eyes from the sun with her hand. "Who's there?" she asked.

Clare caught up to Emmy and placed a hand on her shoulder before they reached the girls. "Em," she whispered. "What's the best way to catch flies?"

Emmy looked at her sister. "With honey." She took a breath, put a smile on her face, and walked calmly over to them.

"Hi, Willy, Abby!" said Clare. "Whatcha doin'?"

"Oh, hey Clare. Hi, Emmy," said Willy.

"Happy Bestie Day!" said Clare.

"Same to you," said Abby.

Emmy forced herself to smile at Willy. "What's with the clippers?"

"You know Abs and I are besties, right?" asked Willy. She didn't wait for an answer. "*Everyone* knows that. We were the first kids our age to have besties. *Anyway*, we're making Bestie Day bouquets for each other!"

"Nice!" said Clare.

Emmy frowned. "Don't you think you've cut enough flowers for bouquets?"

Willy laughed. "Not. Even. Close!"

"Nope!" said Abby.

"I'm the best bestie, right Abs?" said Willy.

"The best!" said Abby.

"So, my bouquet has to be biggest, right Abs?"

"The biggest!" said Abby.

"Buuuzzzz!" Bees circled the cut flowers.

"Bugs!" cried Willy. "Shoo!" She grabbed her swatter, but Emmy put a hand on her arm.

"Hey!" said Willy.

"Sorry, but bees are an important part of

nature," said Emmy. "You shouldn't swat them."

"She's right," said Clare. "Bees spread pollen so plants can reproduce."

"Yeah," said Emmy. "Without the bees, there'd be far fewer flowers."

"Really? I like flowers. Maybe we *should* leave the bees alone," said Abby.

Willy glared at her friend. Abby blushed. "Um . . . that is, if *you* think we should, Willy."

"Fine!" said Willy, handing Emmy the swatter. "But I am *not* done cutting flowers!"

"Willy," said Emmy. "The thing is, the bees need the flowers, too, for food. So, please. Stop cutting them."

"No way!" shouted Willy. "It's Bestie Day,

not Bee-stie Day! And this bestie wants a big bouquet!"

Willy turned back to the flowers, again raising her clippers. Emmy pulled some trillium petals from her pouch. "Wait, Willy, look!" Emmy said. "We collected these beautiful petals *from the ground*. We're going to make really cool crafts with them without cutting any flowers at all. Wanna try? You'd be helping the bees."

Willy rolled her eyes. But Emmy just kept smiling at her.

Finally, Willy gave in. "Fine. We'll pick fallen petals. Right, Abs?"

Abby stared at Willy with wide eyes, but Willy didn't say anything else. Finally, she stammered, "I guess. . . . *If it's okay with you . . .*"

"I just said it was!" snapped Willy.

"Great! Here's a head start," said Emmy.
She dropped some petals into Abby's hand.

"Wow, thanks," Abby said.

Suddenly, Willy turned to Clare. "That

earring you're wearing is pretty cool! It is *so* sparkly."

"Thanks," said Clare.

Then, Willy spotted Emmy's green charm. "Nature girl! You've got one, too?"

"Our dad gave these charms to us," said Emmy.

"Well, I need one—or two or three!" Willy said. "Where'd he get them?"

"Oh, you can't *buy* these," explained Clare.

"Oh yeah?" began Willy. "I get everything I want—" But suddenly she was interrupted.

"Em! Clare! Where are you guys?" they all heard.

"That's Giselle," said Clare.

"We've gotta go." Emmy took Clare's hand

and they ran toward the river.

As soon as they were gone, Willy grabbed the petals from Abby. She dropped them on the ground and crushed them with her heel. "Gifts made from petals? That fell on the ground? That's practically garbage. They have *got* to be kidding!" She grabbed her clippers and started cutting again.

"But what about the bees?" asked Abby.

"Un-bee-lievable! They're bugs, Abs! Who cares? Now help me!"

CHAPTER 7

As Giselle waited for her sisters, she watched Soar played in a patch of flowers at the edge of the field. The little bird hopped to the left of a stem, then to the right, then in a circle all around the flower. *What is she doing?*

Above Soar's head was a little bee. As they mirrored each other's movements, it looked like the bee was dancing with Soar! Giselle

clapped her hands.

"Soar, you made a friend on Bestie Day!"

"*Yip, yip!*" went Soar.

"Well, she needs a name," continued Giselle. "I know! Let's call her Bizzy, cause she's a busy bee!"

"*Woo!*" whistled Soar.

"Glad you like it!" Giselle giggled.

Just then, Clare and Emmy arrived, breathless.

"You guys *ran* here?" asked Giselle.

"Everything okay?"

"I hope so," said Emmy. "We just saw Willy and Abby. They were cutting an awful lot of wildflowers and trying to swat some bees."

"That's not cool!" Giselle said.

"No, but I think we convinced them to collect fallen petals instead," said Clare.

"And another thing," Emmy added. "Willy was really interested in our charms! She wanted to buy one for herself."

"Don't worry." Giselle laughed. "Willy wants *everything*. She'll find something else she wants tomorrow and forget all about the charms."

"I hope so," Emmy replied. "Willy can be

mean when she doesn't get her way."

"Forget Willy. It's Bestie Day! Did you find some petals?" asked Giselle.

"Did we!" Emmy grinned, then opened the pouch hanging from her waist. "Look! Trillium petals in every color!"

"Wow! Slam dunk!" said Giselle. "Hey, that's nice. Where'd you get it?" she asked, gesturing to the pouch.

"Dad made it in case our petal charms combine again," Emmy explained.

"And I turned it into a hands-free holder!" added Clare.

"Sweet!" said Giselle. She grabbed a backpack from the kayak and dropped the petals inside. "Okay, Trills, do we need more petals or are we ready to make gifts?"

"Let's collect one more round," Clare suggested. "Emmy gave a bunch to Abby."

"Cool," said Giselle as she strapped the pack with their gear to her back. "Let me just call Soar. She made a new friend!"

"Uh-oh! That doesn't look good," said Clare. She pointed in the distance to what

looked like a yellow pom-pom. It rose above the wild grass and then dropped back down. Then a pink one did the same.

"Aww, pine cones!" said Emmy. "I hope that's not what I think it is."

"But I think it *is* what you think it is," said Clare.

"Who? Thinks what? I'm confused," said Giselle.

"Those were flowers being thrown onto a pile," Clare explained.

"Which means Willy is still at it," said Emmy.

"Let's be sure." Giselle dropped low and started sneaking through the tall grass toward Abby and Willy. Emmy and Clare followed.

As they got closer, they could see Willy *was* still cutting flowers—and even faster than before.

"Sour flours! She lied to us!" hissed Clare.

"What's that?" whispered Giselle. She pointed to what looked like a small black cloud, hovering over the flower pile.

"Bees," said Clare.

"That can't be bees!" Giselle insisted. "There are so many of them!"

"Well," explained Emmy, "the bees came to drink nectar, but

Abby and Willy are hoarding so many cut flowers in that pile, there aren't enough flowers they can reach!"

"What'll happen if they don't get nectar?" Giselle asked.

"They won't be able to fly! Bees get weak pretty quickly without nectar!" said Emmy.

Suddenly, they heard *Buuuuzzzzzzz!* All the bees zoomed away from the field and into the forest!

"Where are they going?" cried Giselle.

"I think they left to search for other flowers in the forest," said Emmy. "I hope there are some close by."

"Whoa, look!" cried Clare. "Something's hopping after the bees!"

"Aww, beeswax!" said Giselle. "That's Soar! She's following her bee friend, Bizzy. I have to get her, before she gets lost." Giselle took off after her pet.

Clare put two fingers in her mouth and whistled as hard as she could. Claw and Fluffy came running. The sisters scooped up their pets and raced after Giselle, Soar, and the bees.

CHAPTER 8

In the distance, Soar finally stopped. The girls sprinted as fast as their legs would carry them. When they reached her, she was perched on the ground next to Bizzy. The bee was barely moving!

"*Woo! Woo!*" whistled Soar. She hopped into Giselle's arms.

"Don't worry," said Giselle. "We'll help your friend."

Emmy looked around but couldn't believe her eyes. The bees all around them were in a similar state, buzzing weakly on the ground.

"This doesn't look good," said Clare.

"What's wrong with them all?" asked Giselle.

"They ran out of energy before they found any nectar!" Emmy explained.

The group quickly scoured the area, but couldn't find any flowers in this shady patch of forest.

Clare thought for a second. "Can't we feed them the flowers Abby and Willy cut?"

"How? We're too far away from the field now to make that work," said Giselle.

"*Ahoo!*" Fluffy whimpered. He pointed his snout at a group of bees that now lay still on the forest floor. He gently prodded them with his nose, but it didn't wake them.

"This is going from bad to worse fast!" exclaimed Emmy. She started to pace back and forth. "What are we going to do?"

"Calm down, Em," said Clare. "You can't think straight when you're upset."

But Emmy paced even faster. "The bees are so important to life on our mountain. We *have* to save them!" Tears filled her eyes.

"Em," said Clare evenly. "This *is* an emergency, but we'll think of something if we work together." She held out her hands to both sisters.

But Giselle shot to her feet instead. Her mouth hung open, and she pointed with both hands to Emmy's petal charm. The green enamel glistened in the sunshine as the charm lifted off her neck.

Emmy's hand leapt to her chest. "Trills, I think our charms are activating again!" she cried.

Clare's pink petal charm strained toward Emmy's green one. "You're right, Em! I feel it. I feel the magic pulling the charms together," she cried.

Giselle looked down. Her blue charm was tugging toward the others, too.

"C'mon charms, c'mon!" said Clare. "From petals to flower . . ."

". . . make us sisters . . ." said Giselle.

". . . with power!" finished Emmy.

And that did it—*Zoom!* The petal charms flew together and fused into one beautiful, seamless trillium flower charm that glowed as if lit from within. Then, a blinding light fired off the flower charm, touching the mini'mals. *Whoosh!* The mini'mals shot up into full-size animals—a huge, strong, eagle, bear, and wolf! And then—*Fwomp!*—the whole forest shimmered, and the girls were transformed. Now, they were dressed in warrior wear.

"We did it! We're sisters with power!" cried Giselle.

"Now we can save these bees, Trills!" said Emmy.

Clare swung into action. She used her super vision to scan through the forest all the way into the field, where she spotted Willy. "There are still flowers left, Trills. But we need to stop Willy before it's too late!"

CHAPTER 9

As the girls prepared the maxi'mals to return to the flower field, Emmy remembered the pouch her father had given her. She grabbed the glowing trillium flower charm and stored it safely. Then she jumped onto Claw's back. "Go, Claw! To the field!" she cried.

The huge bear reared up on her hind legs. *"Ahooo!"* As her howl rang through the forest, she took off!

Clare jumped onto Fluffy's back with a "*Heeeya!*" The powerful wolf sprinted after them.

Soar, now a mighty eagle, tipped her head and Giselle dove onto her back. "Up!" she cried. But Soar hesitated. She turned back toward the bees.

"Don't worry. We'll get nectar for Bizzy," said Giselle. "We'll save *all* the bees, but we have to hurry! So, fly! Fly!"

With that, Soar leapt forward, pumped her powerful wings, and rose into the air.

Above the tree line, the sun baked Giselle's shoulders and the warm air dried her throat. If she felt this thirsty, she could only imagine how badly those poor bees needed nectar. "Hurry, Soar!" she cried.

As the flower field came into view, Giselle saw she had arrived first. *I have to get those cut flowers for the bees. But Abby and Willy can't see me take them!* She spotted a group of bushes tall enough to hide Soar from view. "Down," she directed. The eagle glided to a soft landing right behind the bushes.

"Good, girl. Now stay," Giselle said. She climbed off Soar's back and stowed her backpack by the bush.

Giselle scanned the field, searching for trees along the way to hide herself from view. With her route set to retrieve the flowers, she took a deep breath before taking off for the first tree. It was about half a football field away. But she reached it twice as fast as she expected! She'd never run that fast before. Did her super strength mean she could run superfast, too?

She focused on the next tree. It was farther—an entire football field away. *Deep breath. Ready, set, go!*

Again, she arrived much faster than normal. Giselle pumped an arm in silent victory. *Yaaasss!* Now, knowing how quickly she could move undetected, she took off, zipping from tree to tree, until she reached the flower pile. Giselle grabbed as many flowers as she could, then sprinted back to Soar.

"Did you hear something?" Willy asked looking up from the flower she was cutting.

Abby looked around. "Nope. Maybe it was the wind?"

Giselle returned faster than Emmy or Clare expected. "Trills, you are not gonna believe this, but my super strength makes me superfast, too!"

"Super cool!" said Clare.

"I can fetch the rest of the flowers and fly them to the bees in no time!" Giselle beamed.

"Thank goodness!" Emmy replied. She threw her arms around her sister.

"And *we'll* stop Willy and Abby from cutting more flowers," said Clare. "If we don't, then more bees will be harmed."

"Right! Together, we'll get it done," Emmy added. "Here's to the power of three!"

With the plan in place, Giselle confidently sprinted back to collect the rest of the flowers. She grabbed them and returned, but back at the bushes, she suddenly felt dizzy.

Clare wrapped an arm around her sister to steady her.

"Whoa, I don't know what's wrong . . ." began Giselle.

"I do!" said Emmy. She grabbed a granola bar and broke it into pieces, and held one out. "It's past lunchtime. You need food, just like the bees!"

"Em's right," said Clare. "Sit and eat. *I'll* figure out how to carry all these flowers to the bees."

Clare looked around. There wasn't

anything to hold so many blooms except . . . the backpack! She dumped their supplies under the bushes, then tucked flowers into every available space in the pack. When she was done, it looked like an enormous bouquet of wildflowers!

Giselle stood up. "I'm much better now. Thanks, Em."

"And the flowers are ready to roll," said Clare. Giselle strapped on her pack and hopped onto Soar's back. Then the mighty eagle, covered in blossoms, lifted into the clear blue sky.

CHAPTER 10

With Giselle off on her mission, Emmy lifted the glowing charm from her pouch to check on it. The girls had learned last time that their magic lasted only as long as the trillium charm glowed. She was relieved to see it still glimmering brightly, but Emmy knew that once it started to fade, they'd have very little time before their powers disappeared. "Clare, we have to get moving!"

"Abso-trilly! Time to spy with my power-ful eye!" said Clare. She aimed her super vision toward the flower field. "Willy's *still* cutting, but Abby looks tired."

"Hmmm. Do you think Abby would help

us convince Willy to stop?" Emmy wondered.

"Worth a try," said Clare.

Emmy and Clare jumped on their maxis and sprinted toward the other girls.

Meanwhile, Willy noticed flowers strewn about her feet. "Abs," she called. "You're too slow! Catch faster, and put them in our pile!"

Abby sighed. Her back ached from all the bending. *Isn't Bestie Day supposed to be fun? Maybe we have enough flowers now.* She turned to look at the blooms they'd already cut. "Ahhhh!" she cried.

"What?" said Willy. "Is it a bug?!"

"No, the flowers!" said Abby. "They're gone!"

"That's not even possible," Willy insisted. But as she turned, her mouth dropped open. "Ahhhh! My flowers are gone!" She glared at Abby. "What'd you do with them?"

"What'd *I* do with them?" said Abby.

"Flowers don't just disappear!"

"So it's my fault?"

"Maybe you hid them!" said Willy, narrowing her eyes.

"Why would I do *that*?" Abby asked.

"Because—" But then, Willy froze. She stared over Abby's head off into the field.

"What is it?" said Abby, tugging at Willy's arm.

"Someone's coming! I can't make out who

it is, but *they* must have taken our flowers."
She stomped her foot. "Oooo, are they gonna
be sorry!"

"Willy, hold on. Let's *ask* if they took the
flowers first. . . ."

"Abs, there's no one else around! They
must be the flower theives! C'mon!" Willy
started to run toward Clare and Emmy.
"Heeeyyyyy!"

Fluffy's ears pricked up. Even though he
looked like a big wolf, inside he was still a
puppy and loud noise frightened him. As the
screaming came closer, he reared up.

"Fluffy, no!" cried Clare, but it was too
late. The wolf stumbled back, fell on his
bottom, and burped.

Suddenly, a white fog appeared everywhere! Thick as pea soup, it blanketed the field, settling on the ground and turning the dirt to mud.

Claw dug her sharp nails into the field and skidded to a stop near Fluffy. Emmy grabbed her bear's fur so she didn't slide off. "Whoa! You okay, Clare?" asked Emmy.

"Uh-huh. I hung on. But . . . what just happened?"

"No idea!" Emmy whispered in response.

"Abby?" cried Willy. "I can't see in this fog and I'm sliiiiiiipping!"

"Me too!" called Abby.

And then—*Swish!*

"Yuuuuuuck!" howled Willy. "I'm muddy!"

"Ugh! I am, too," complained Abby. She

started to giggle.

"Not! Funny!" screamed Willy.

"A little funny," Abby replied through her laughter.

"Ahh, a bug! A slimy bug!" cried Willy.

Emmy felt Clare's hand on her shoulder. "I can see through the fog with my super vision," she whispered. "C'mon, I'll get us someplace safe."

Clare shepherded the maxis and Emmy to a thick grove of trees. When they were out of earshot, she whispered again, "Good thing that fog rolled in! It stopped Abby and Willy."

"But now what?" asked Emmy.

"I'm not sure," said Clare. "Willy and Abby can't see to cut flowers in this fog but it *will* clear. Plus, I see a bunch of flowers got damaged when they slipped. Now there's even fewer healthy plants."

"Oh, no. That's not good for the bees."

"Nope."

The girls were quiet as they thought.

Finally, Emmy said, "Clare, remember how I healed Zee's cuts with my magic when he fell in the river?"

"Yeah, that was incredible."

"This might sound like a long shot . . . but . . . do you think my healing might work on plants, too?"

Clare looked at her sister with wide eyes. "No clue . . . but let's try!"

Clare led Emmy to the injured plants.

They looked terrible. Leaves hung limply from stems, and roots dangled in the air. Clare guided Emmy's finger to the plant and held her breath.

She gasped at what she saw next! As Emmy touched the stem, the plant sparkled, and the roots dove back into the soil! Then, the whole plant pulled upright, the flowers reaching skyward once more.

"Em, that finger of yours is bee-utiful!" whispered Clare.

"C'mon, let's heal them all!" replied Emmy.

Clare guided Emmy's finger, and one by one, they rerooted all the plants. Then, the girls returned to Fluffy and Claw.

"That was amazing, but I still don't get where this fog came from . . . or when it's going to lift." Clare frowned.

"*Ahoo!*" howled Fluffy softly.

"Shhh, Fluff," said Clare. "Willy and Abby might hear you."

But Fluffy didn't stop. He pawed at Clare's leg. She knelt down to beside him. "What's wrong?" she said gently. Fluffy looked right back at her—and burped in her face!

"Ewww! Bad boy!" But then, suddenly, it clicked! A little fresh fog had escaped

Fluffy's lips when he burped. Emmy couldn't have seen it, but with her super vision, Clare watched the new fog emerge and swirl into the old, like a magic potion mixing together.

"Emmy!" whispered Clare. "You're not going to believe this, but . . . I think Fluffy has a magic power, too! *He* made the fog!"

"What? How?"

Clare grinned. "By burping!"

"This is no time for jokes," said Emmy, annoyed. "Burping is *not* a magic power."

"I know! But Fluffy's burp makes us invisible, and that's a magic power." Clare jumped to her feet. "We'll use the fog to stop Willy and Abby for good and save every bee on this mountain! C'mon!"

CHAPTER 11

When Clare had perfectly positioned Claw and Fluffy, she whispered to Claw, "Dig, girl, dig!" Then she grabbed Emmy's hand and walked confidently through the fog in the other direction, away from Abby and Willy.

"Hey, Em!" said Clare in a loud voice, over her shoulder. "We came back for a few more trillium petals, but check out those wild geraniums over there! Aren't they gorgeous?"

Willy hissed at Abby, "How can she see flowers in this fog? I can't even see my own hand in front of my face!"

"Beats me. But the mud is fun! Wanna make a mud pie?" asked Abby.

"Gross! No!" Willy replied. "Plus, if there are geraniums over there, I need 'em for my bouquet."

"*Your* bouquet?" Abby replied.

"I mean *our* bouquets. C'mon." She yanked Abby to her feet.

Claw gave a low deep growl. "*Grrrrrr!*"

"What was that?" said Abby in a shaky voice.

Clare glanced back over her shoulder. "The hole is ready," whispered Clare. Then, more loudlly, she called, "Those geraniums are just ahead, Em. Let's go see them up close."

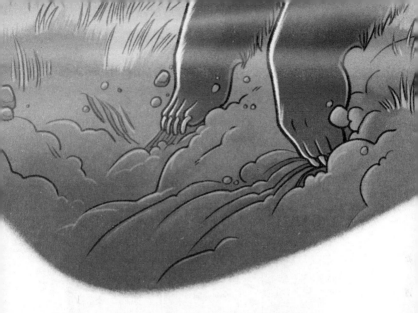

"Go on, Abs," whispered Willy. "You want those flowers!" She gave Abby a little shove.

Abby lurched forward—and tumbled into the hole! "Ahhh!" she cried.

Willy lost her footing, too, and slid down into the hole after her.

"Yuck! Now I'm even muddier!" cried Willy. "This was your worst plan ever!"

"*My* plan? *You* wanted more flowers! I wanted to make mud pies!"

"So?"

"So!"

"Stop touching me with your slimy fingers!" Willy complained.

"I'm not. It's probably a worm," Abby shouted back.

"EWWWW!"

Clare plugged her ears. She couldn't think with all that racket. But when she looked down to concentrate, her heart began to race. The trillium flower charm in Emmy's pouch was starting to fade! That meant their powers would soon be gone! The sisters had to finish what they'd started or the bees would never truly be safe!

CHAPTER 12

As Giselle soared toward the bees, she marveled at how beautiful the mountain was from the sky. It looked like a blanket of green, speckled with dots of red, pink, yellow, and purple. Giselle knew the dots were clusters of wildflowers and seemed tiny only because she flew so far above them.

Suddenly, her palms started to sweat. The

flowers were tiny dots! How would she find even tinier bees on the forest floor if she couldn't even make out flowers from way up here? Last time she'd flown on Soar to save her father, Clare's super vision had made it easy for them to locate him on the ground, but Giselle was alone now.

She forced herself to take three long, even breaths. She could hear Clare encouraging her. She'd find a solution if she just kept calm. Aha! The bees had been looking for food, but hadn't been able to find any. That meant they couldn't be near the colored dots, which were flowers. They had to be in the spaces that were solid green.

When the next span of green appeared,

Giselle commanded, "Down, girl, down!" and Soar lowered her head and dove through the trees. Unfortunately, Giselle didn't see any bees as they neared the forest floor.

"Up, Soar, up!" she cried, and Soar lifted her head and shot back up to the sky like a rocket on liftoff. The air pushed against Giselle's face. "Woohoo!" she called out.

It took three tries but Giselle finally found the fallen bees.

"Down, girl!" cried Giselle. "I hope we got here in time!"

The mighty eagle glided in to a clearing. As Soar's talons touched the ground, Giselle jumped off her back and sprinted to the first group of bees, pulling flowers from her pack and placing them carefully on the forest floor. But the bees didn't move. *Was I gone too long? Are they too weak to even drink?*

Giselle felt tears burn her eyes. She dropped her head and knelt on the ground. *"Woo! Woo!"* whistled Soar gently. Giselle looked at her eagle. *Nature is depending on me. I have to keep trying.*

She ran to Bizzy, scooped her up in a leaf, and tilted her toward an open flower. Finally, Bizzy drank! And drank and drank. Then she fluttered her wings and slowly hovered at the flower bud on her own.

Giselle raced from group to group, helping other bees drink the same way. And as the other bees watched her help their friends, they copied, drinking from the flowers she'd laid near them. Soon, the forest floor was buzzing again. Giselle had never heard a sweeter sound.

CHAPTER 13

Back at the flower field, the trillium charm was fading by the second.

"Aaaaabby!" screamed Willy.

"I'm right here! Stop screaming!" screamed Abby.

"The fog is lighter . . . and I can see a spider in the hole!" cried Willy, pushing back against the wall.

"So?"

"So!"

"Clare," whispered Emmy, "if the fog clears, they'll see our glowing charm."

"I know! We gotta get out of here!" Clare put her arms around the maxis' necks and jogged them away from the hole. Emmy followed in the nick of time.

Poof! The three petal charms separated, softly jingling against one another, in the bottom of the pouch.

Poof! The maxi'mals shrank back to mini size! *"Ahoo,"* whined Claw. Emmy lifted her onto her hip.

Pop! The fog disappeared.

Pfft! Emmy and Clare were back in their

normal clothes.

"Help!" cried Willy. "Is anybody there? I'm stuck in a wormy spider pit!"

Clare and Emmy looked at each other. They motioned for the minis to stay behind the trees, then jogged back toward the hole.

"Willy? Abby! We heard you call. Are you okay?" asked Clare.

"Yes," said Abby.

"No!" cried Willy. "There's worms!"

"Don't worry," said Emmy. "Worms are super nice. And, they're good for the dirt!"

"Get me out of here, you nature nuts!" Willy demanded.

Clare offered a hand, but Willy grabbed on so desperately, Clare almost fell in, too.

"Hold on." Clare calmly lay on her stomach and helped Willy climb out. "How'd you wind up in there?"

"We didn't see the hole," Abby explained.

"Yeah, that fog was super weird," agreed Emmy. She extended a hand to Abby, who

easily made it out with her help.

Back on solid ground, Willy looked around frantically.

"What's wrong? Did you lose something?" Clare asked.

"Our flowers! We cut a huge pile of them, but they're gone!"

Emmy stepped forward so she was face-to-face with Willy. "But you told me you'd use fallen petals for Bestie Day gifts."

Willy stared at Emmy, opening her mouth but no words came out. She turned toward Abby. "We . . . well . . . ummm."

Finally, Abby spoke up. "We *wanted* to use fallen petals to make gifts, but we didn't know how."

"Well then, dancing daisies, it's your lucky

day!" said Clare. "*We* know how."

"Of course you do," grumbled Willy.

"We brought supplies with us for flower gifts," Emmy added. "We left them by those bushes. Want to see?"

"Yes!" said Abby.

"No," said Willy.

Clare and Emmy ran toward the cluster of bushes. Abby followed close behind.

"Don't leave me with the bugs!" cried Willy, racing after them.

When the girls got to the thicket, Clare reached underneath to retrieve the supplies. She laid the plastic bowl, the flower press, and the needle and thread on the grass.

"Now what would you two like to make— perfume, a dried-flower bookmark, or a flower hat?" Emmy asked.

"They all sound cool to me!" said Abby. "Willy, you pick."

"I've got a million hats at home," complained Willy. "And what am I doing to do with *dried* flowers?"

Clare smiled brightly. "Then perfume it is!"

"Good idea," agreed Abby. "We smell like mud. Smelling like perfume would be way better!"

"*I* don't smell like mud," grumbled Willy. Abby wrinkled her nose before looking at Emmy, then covered her mouth with a hand as she giggled.

Clare grabbed a smooth stone from the ground and showed the girls how to mash the petals so the fragrant oil collected in the bowl. Then, she added water to the bowl and swirled it around.

As the sweet smell wafted into the air, a few bees flew over to investigate.

"Look!" cried Emmy. "The bees like it!"

"No more bees!" Willy whined.

Clare snapped a lid on the bowl and the bees flitted away. She handed the container to Abby. "Happy Bestie Day!"

"You mean we can *keep* this?" said Abby.

"Abso-trilly!" Emmy replied.

"Wow, thanks!" said Abby. "C'mon, Willy. Let's clean up and put on perfume."

"Fine," grumbled Willy, shuffling after Abby.

CHAPTER 14

Once Willy and Abby were out of sight, Clare and Emmy exchanged a high-five. They'd done it! They'd stopped Willy from cutting any more flowers!

But their relief was temporary. What had happened to the bees in the forest?

"Do you think Giselle made it to them in time?" Emmy wondered. "I'm so worried about Bizzy and the other bees, my stomach is doing flip-flops."

"I hope so," said Clare. "But the only way to know for sure is to find Giselle. C'mon!"

Emmy and Clare scooped up their pets and hiked out of the field and into the forest. With the magic gone, they knew Giselle would be walking, too. They kept a steady course, hoping to meet her in the middle.

Finally, Emmy saw her in the distance. "There's our sis, sis!" she cried. She broke into a run.

"Giselle!" called Emmy. "Did it work? Did you save them?"

Giselle threw open her arms, and the sisters ran into a terrifically tight triplet hug.

"Bull's-eye, Besties! Our plan worked! The bees are buzzing! How'd *you* guys do?"

"Bee-utiful! Abby and Willy finally agreed to make gifts from fallen petals," said Emmy. "I think Abby truly wanted to help the bees."

"But not Willy," said Clare. "She just didn't get it."

"Then how'd you stop her?" asked Giselle.

"It was Fluffy!" said Emmy. "He burped out white fog and while Abby and Willy couldn't see, Claw dug a pit, and we trapped them in it!"

"It was *so* cool!" added Clare.

"The magic makes Fluffy a huge, strong wolf," said Giselle. "Are you telling me he has *another* power, too?"

"Yup!" Emmy confirmed.

"Wow! That is off the mountain!" Giselle cheered.

Clare got a look like she was hatching another idea. "Trills," she said slowly. "Do you think our other pets might have powers, too? Ones we haven't discovered yet?"

"Maybe," said Emmy. "There's still a lot to

learn about our magic."

"There is," agreed Giselle. "But not today. It's Bestie Day! It's time to make those gifts."

Emmy frowned. "Awww, pine cones! I gave the perfume supplies to Abby. That means we don't have a gift for you, Clare."

Clare threw her arms around both sisters and pulled them close. "Who cares? Bestie Day is about best friends. And I've got plenty of those."

Giselle grinned at her sisters. "Me too. I don't need a gift when I have you two."

"Me three!" agreed Emmy. "You two, Dad, and Zee are the best gift ever!"

"Ooh, I miss Dad and Zee!" said Clare. "Do you want to spend the rest of Bestie Day with the whole family?"

"One hundred percent! Let's meet in the Grove," Giselle suggested. "I've got to return the kayak first, though."

"You wanna zip with me, Clare?" said Emmy.

"I thought you'd never ask!"

CHAPTER 15

When the girls arrived at Aspen Grove, Emmy breathlessly recounted all that had happened.

"It was wild!" said Emmy. "The bees were getting weaker and weaker, and Abby and Willy wouldn't stop cutting flowers! It was a double emergency!"

"Which made the charms activate!" Clare explained.

"And *that* gave us the power to save them both!" Giselle added.

Dr. J.A. looked at the girls. His chest swelled and tears stung his eyes. "I'm so proud of you three. By saving the bees, you gave a Bestie Day gift to *everyone* on this mountain!"

"Thanks, Dad," said Clare. "But we couldn't have convinced Willy and Abby to stop cutting flowers without you! *You* taught us that all living things depend on one another."

"What can I say?" Their dad chuckled. "I'm a nature nut!"

"We learned from the best," said Giselle.

"I'm proud to be nature nutty!" Zee giggled.

"And Dad, you were right," said Emmy.

"Even though there was an emergency, we had the power of three—and that was enough."

"Plus, we learned even more about our magic!" added Giselle.

Dr. J.A. nodded. "Which will only make you fiercer when the charms combine next time."

Emmy winked at her dad. Now, the thought of the charms combining seemed exciting. With their power, there was so much good the sisters could do.

Clare raised her water bottle. "I'm thirsty. But let's toast before we drink. To the bees!"

"Buzz—ah!" said the others.

The girls tipped back their heads, but their

bottles were empty. Dr. J.A. jumped up. "You girls need to hydrate after a day like today—and a late lunch isn't a bad idea either. I'm going to run home and grab a picnic for all of us. You watch your brother." Then their dad dashed down the mountain.

Zee got up and stepped behind an aspen tree, returning with his hands behind his back. "Trills, I made you something for Bestie Day! Ta-da!"

He whipped out a large drawing. In it, the triplets stood at the center with their dad and Zee on either side. Surrounding the family were forest animals—moose, deer, squirrels, blue jays, even bees. At the edges of the picture, Zee had drawn a garland of every kind of flower that grew on the mountain.

"Awesome, bro—thank you!" said Giselle.

"We'll hang it in our room as soon as we get back," added Clare.

"So we can see it every day," said Emmy. "How'd you decide what to draw?"

"I drew everyone who loves you," Zee explained. "Especially me!"

The girls hugged their brother as Dr. J.A. returned with a huge picnic basket. He spread a blanket on the ground, and the family enjoyed peanut butter and wild-berry sandwiches, apple salad, and daisy juice. There were even flower cookies for dessert.

Emmy looked up. The sun was beginning to set. As the sky dimmed, a throng of fireflies

flitted around the top of the largest aspen in the Grove. Illuminated, it looked just like a lighthouse.

"Zee," said Emmy. "We have a Bestie Day gift for you, too! Guess what? We've got enough people to play Lighthouse!"

"Ooo! Can we? Can we?" cried Zee. He bounced up and down.

"I can't think of a better way to end Bestie Day," said Dr. J.A.

Giselle tossed Zee up in the air. Then she caught him and carried him to the foot of the tree. "You get to be lighthouse keeper first!"

"Yaasss!" cried Zee. He pumped an arm in the air.

Zee closed his eyes and began to chant:

"From me, the keeper, hide your face.

To win the game, duck, hide, and race.

Crawl on the ground, from tree to tree.

Reach the light, but don't be seen.

Ready, set, GO!"

As the brilliant orange sun fell below the horizon the girls and their father scampered into the darkness.